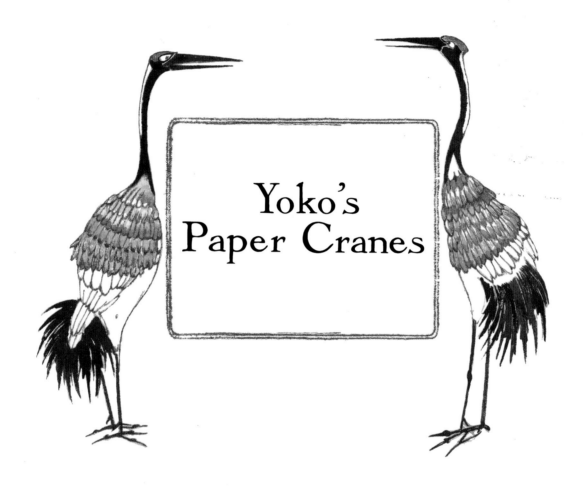

Yoko's
Paper Cranes

Yoko's Paper Cranes

ROSEMARY WELLS

Disney • HYPERION BOOKS
NEW YORK

For information address Disney • Hyperion Books, 114 Fifth Avenue,
New York, New York 10011-5690.

First Disney • Hyperion paperback edition, 2009

1 3 5 7 9 10 8 6 4 2

Library of Congress Cataloging-in-Publication Data on file

ISBN 978-1-4231-1984-5

Visit www.hyperionbooksforchildren.com

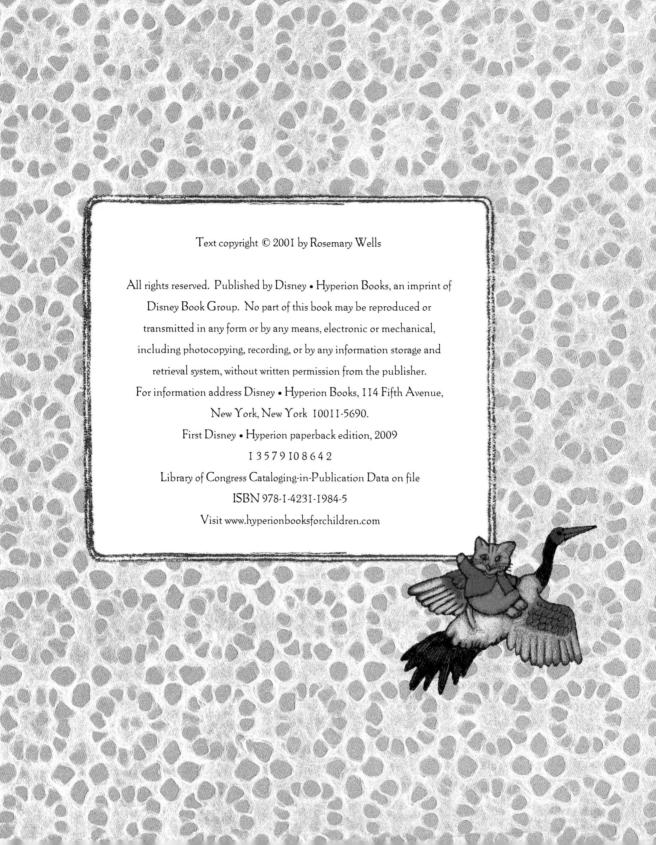

I wish to thank Johanna Hurley, my codesigner
and Master Cutter of Japanese paper.

W hen Yoko was very small, she
and her grandmother, Obaasan, fed the cranes
in the pond at the end of the garden.

"The cranes stay in our garden only
a few months," said Obaasan to Yoko.
"Then they fly away from Japan."

"Don't go," said Yoko.

"The cranes come back every year,"

said Obaasan.

Yoko's grandfather, Ojiisan, taught her
to fold paper into cranes.

Ojiisan made cranes, frogs, and lots of other animals out of his colored papers.

When Yoko was a big girl, she and her mama and papa
sailed far away from Japan.

But Yoko never forgot Obaasan and Ojiisan.

Every week a letter came to Yoko
and her family in America.

Every week a letter went back to
Obaasan and Ojiisan in Japan.

Obaasan's birthday was in winter.

Yoko had no money to buy a birthday present.

Yoko knew that thousands of miles away in Japan, Obaasan's garden was cold and snowy.

Obaasan was waiting for the cranes to come back to her garden pond.

Yoko asked her mother for beautiful paper.
She folded the paper into a crane,
just as Ojiisan had shown her.

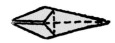

She made three cranes of different colors.

Then she put them in a package

and put stamps on the package.

The mailman took it and sent it in an airplane across the sea.

All night that airplane flew,
from warm California to wintry Japan.

Another mailman left the package at
Obaasan's door.
Obaasan opened the package.

She and Ojiisan hung Yoko's cranes
in the kitchen window.

Obaasan opened Yoko's birthday card.

It was written in Japanese.

"Soon I will come back to Japan, just like the cranes,"
is what the card said.

The paper cranes turned on their strings.

"Happy birthday from Yoko"

tingled in the air around the cranes.